IR

S0-DSN-795

Cat Stats

Sphynx

NICKI CLAUSEN-GRACE

BLACK RABBIT BOOKS

Bolt is published by Black Rabbit Books
P.O. Box 3263, Mankato, Minnesota, 56002.
www.blackrabbitbooks.com
Copyright © 2020 Black Rabbit Books

Jennifer Besel, editor; Catherine Cates,
interior designer; Grant Gould, cover designer;
Omay Ayres, photo researcher

Library of Congress Cataloging-in-Publication Data
Names: Clausen-Grace, Nicki, author.
Title: Sphynx / by Nicki Clausen-Grace.
Description: Mankato, Minnesota : Black Rabbit Books, [2020] |
Series: Bolt. Cat stats | Audience: Age 8-12. | Audience: Grade 4 to 6. |
Includes bibliographical references and index.
Identifiers: LCCN 2018025807 (print) | LCCN 2018028347 (ebook) |
ISBN 9781680728088 (e-book) | ISBN 9781680728026 (library binding) |
ISBN 978644660195 (paperback)
Subjects: LCSH: Sphynx cat—Juvenile literature.
Classification: LCC SF449.S68 (ebook) | LCC SF449.S68 C53 2020 (print) |
DDC 636.8—dc23
LC record available at https://lccn.loc.gov/2018025807

Printed in the United States of America. 1/19

Image Credits
animalchannel.co: sallystrose,
22–23; Shutterstock: Alex Zotov, 3;
alexavol, 19 (m); casey christopher, 26–
27; CJansuebsri, 20–21 (bkgd all images);
cynoclub, 15; Daria Gorbunova, 10 (t); Elena
Butinova, 19 (l); Eric Isselee, Cover, 19 (r), 20–21
(adolescent & adult), 31; FLUKY FLUKY, 14; Indigo
Fish, 17 (t); Juice Team, 32; Konjushenko Vladimir,
1; Kuznetsov Alexey, 20; LaruelleSphotography, 28;
Mikhail Reshetnikov, 24; Mikhail Serebrennikov, 18;
NataliTerr, 4–5; otsphoto, 6–7, 12; SV_zt, 10 (b);
teena137, 14–15 (toy); Triff, 17 (b); Utekhina
Anna, 8–9; Vall Rade, 13; YuliyaRazukevichus,
20–21 (senior)
Every effort has been made to contact
copyright holders for material reproduced
in this book. Any omissions will be
rectified in subsequent printings
if notice is given to
the publisher.

Contents

Meet the

A boy snuggles in bed on a cold morning. His sphynx cat jumps onto the bed. Then it snuggles under the covers too. The boy and his cat are both toasty warm.

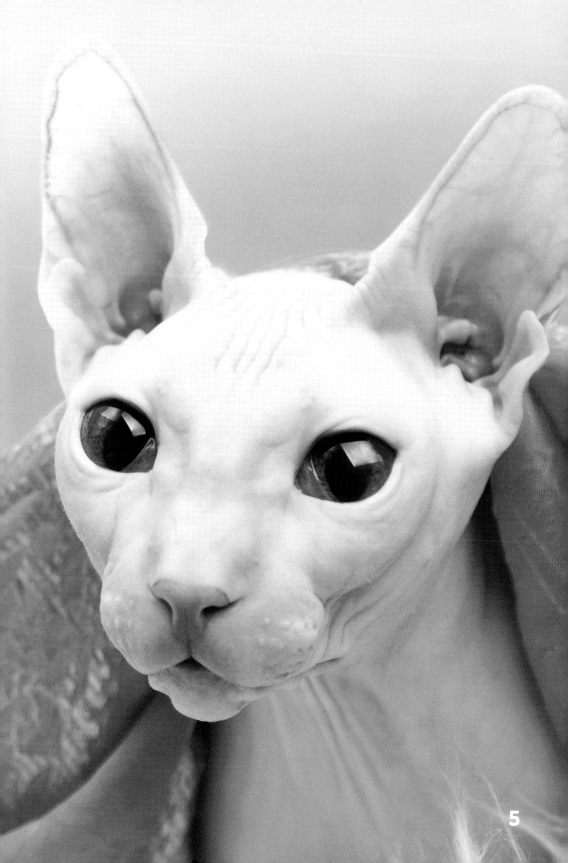

Sphynx were
originally called
Canadian
Hairless cats.

6

Sphynx History

Sphynx cats are known for their hairless bodies and big ears. Their unusual look came from a surprise **genetic mutation**. In 1966, a shorthair cat in Canada gave birth to a hairless kitten. The owner then **bred** the hairless cat to create more hairless kittens. That's how the sphynx **breed** began.

PARTS OF A SPHYNX

BIG EYES

WHIPLIKE TAIL

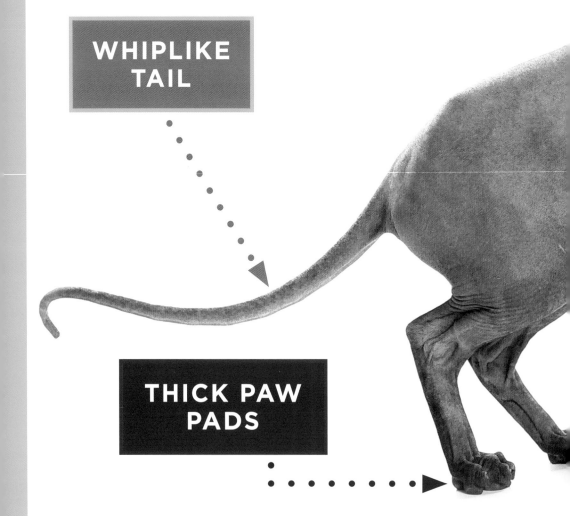

THICK PAW PADS

VERY
LARGE
EARS

**WRINKLED
SKIN**

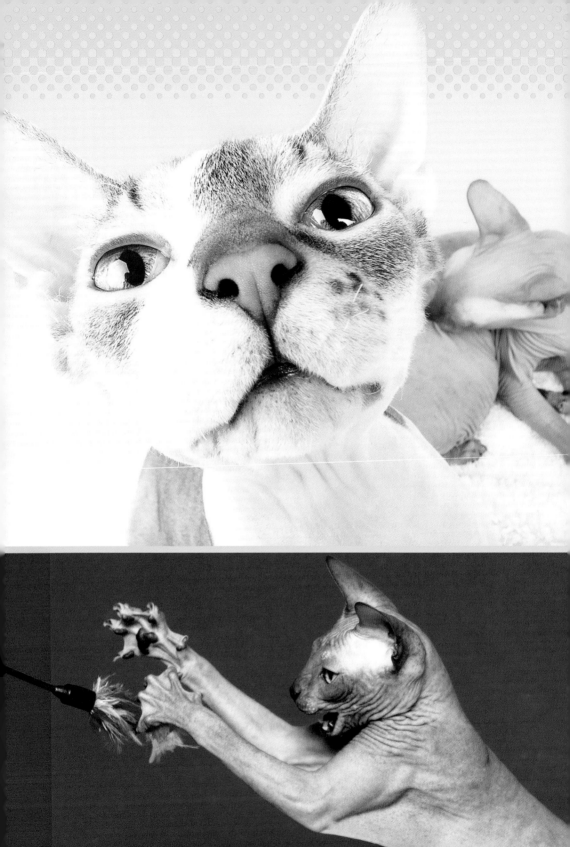

CHAPTER 2

A Special  Personality

Some movies show sphynx as evil characters. But nothing could be more untrue. Sphynx cats are very loving. They like to be held, petted, and played with. They are curious and smart too.

Loves Company

Sphynx love to be the center of attention. They don't like being alone for long periods of time. They want to be with their owners. Other cats and dogs also make good company.

These cats love to be warm.
They curl up with their owners whenever they can.

Tons of Energy

Sphynx have a lot of energy. They are strong, **athletic**, and love to climb. Owners often find them on high shelves.

Owners keep their sphynx busy with puzzle or teaser games. Some puzzle toys let cats move balls around tracks. Teaser toys give cats something to chase.

CHAPTER 3

Sphynx's

Sphynx definitely have a **unique** look. They come in all kinds of colors and patterns. They can be solid colors, such as black or white. Or they can have patterned skin with spots or color patches.

Sphynx look hairless, but they do actually have a little hair. A short fuzz grows on their bodies.

COMPARING
SIZES

Size

Sphynx are medium-sized cats. They weigh between 6 and 12 pounds (3 and 5 kilograms). They might look **fragile**, but they are not. These cats have strong muscles and bones.

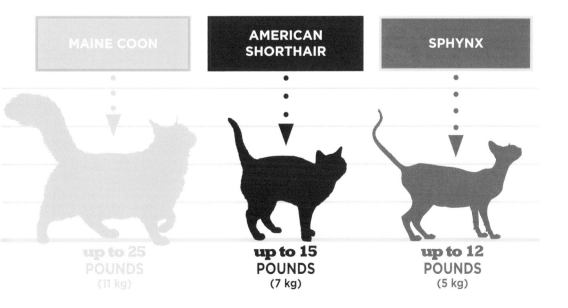

MAINE COON

AMERICAN SHORTHAIR

SPHYNX

up to 25 POUNDS (11 kg)

up to 15 POUNDS (7 kg)

up to 12 POUNDS (5 kg)

Sphynx

Life Cycle

Kittens learn to climb, run, and jump.

KITTEN

Older sphynx move a little slower. These cats live up to 15 years.

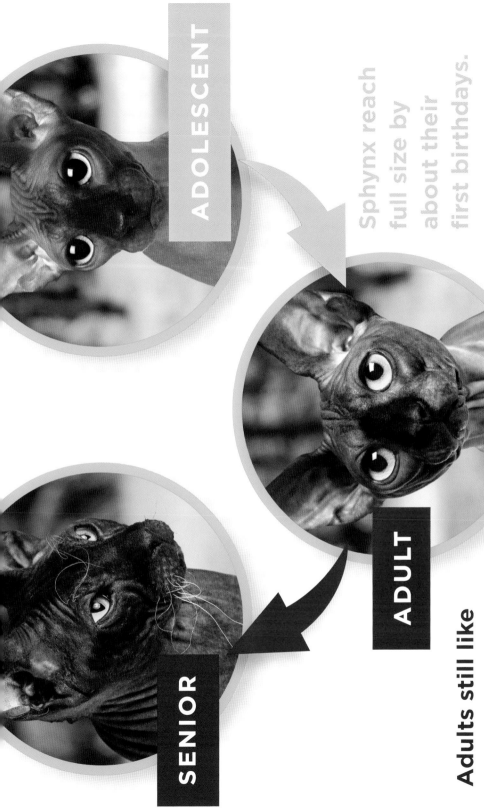

ADOLESCENT

Sphynx reach full size by about their first birthdays.

ADULT

Adults still like to play.

SENIOR

CHAPTER 4

Caring

for a Sphynx

Like all cats, sphynx need regular care. These cats eat a lot of food. They also need water and a clean litter box every day.

Because they have little hair, body **oils** collect on their skin. These cats need a weekly bath to wash away the oils. It is a good idea to brush their teeth weekly too.

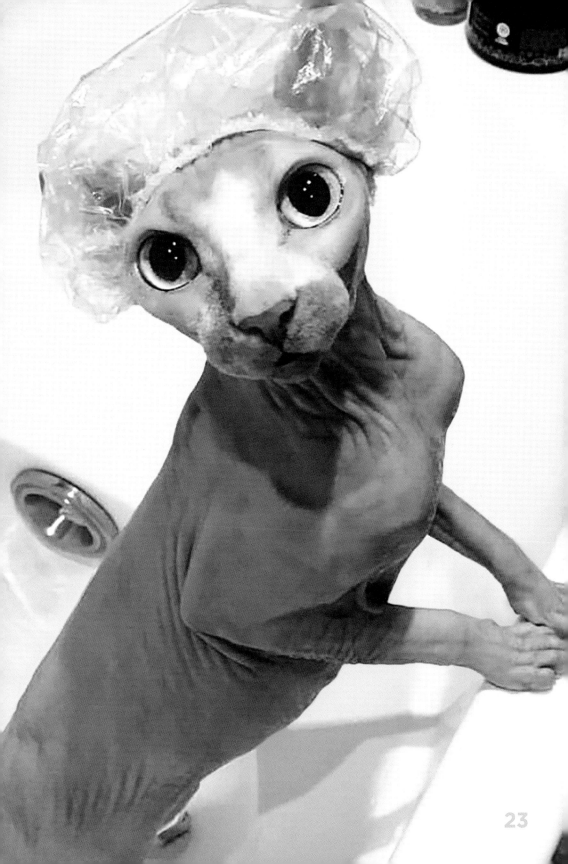

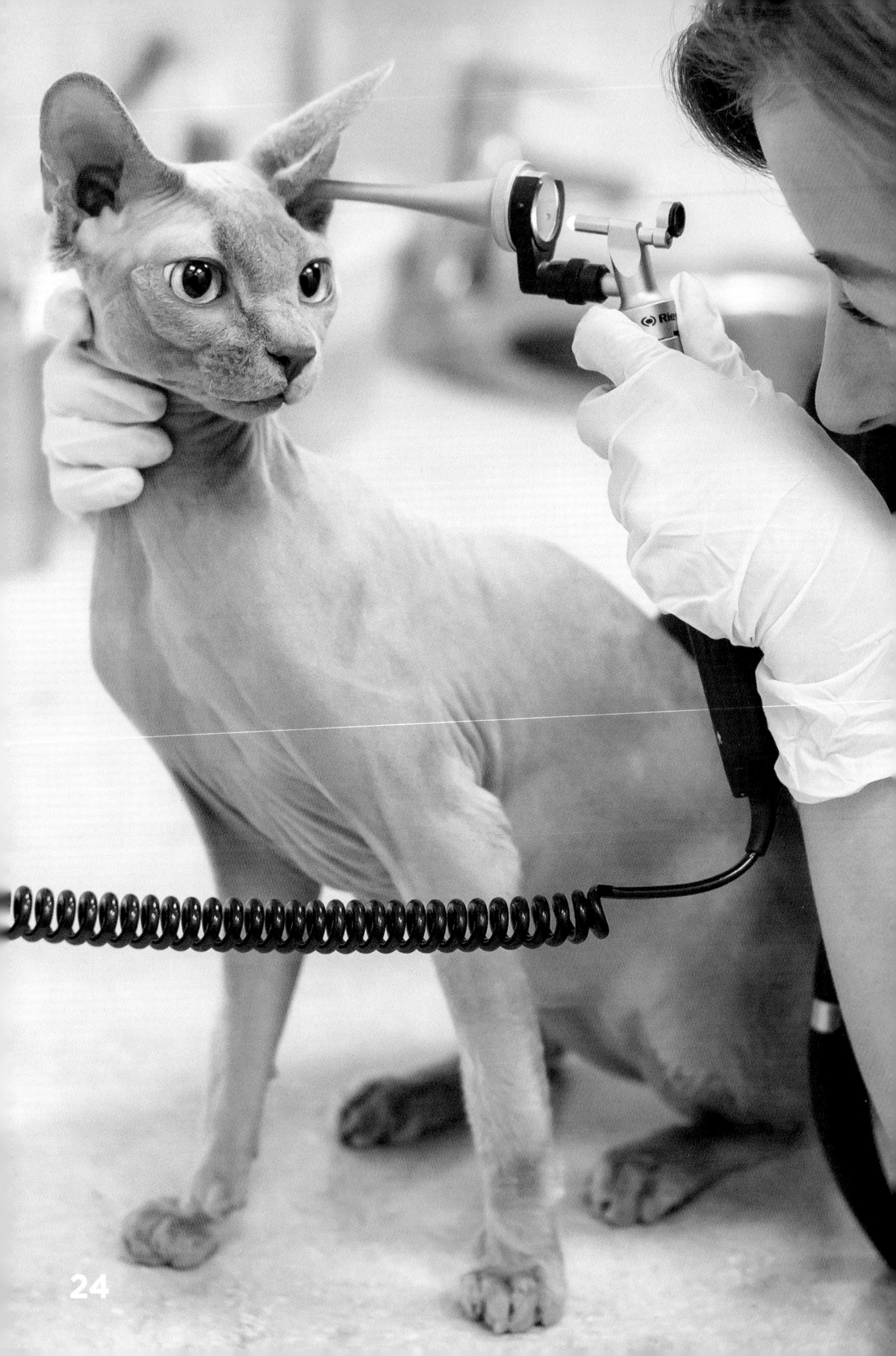

Health Problems

Sphynx are usually healthy. One problem to watch for is skin **infections**. They also can have heart or muscle problems. Regular visits to the vet can help keep them healthy.

Sphynx can get sunburned. They shouldn't spend much time in the sun.

Loveable Friend

Sphynx cats are smart and playful. They love spending time with their owners. A sphynx can be a good addition to a family. These cats are popular pets. And it's not hard to see why.

Is a Sphynx

Answer the questions below. Then add up your points to see if a sphynx is a good fit.

1 **Do you like a fluffy cat?**

A. I want to cuddle with a ball of fur. (1 point)

B. It feels nice to pet fur. (2 points)

C. I don't need all that fur. (3 points)

2 **Do you want a cat that doesn't need much attention?**

A. I'm too busy to play with my cat all the time. **(1 point)**

B. I need a cat that can be happy alone sometimes. (2 points)

C. I am looking for a constant companion. **(3 points)**

3 **Do you want a cat that looks like most other cats?**

A. I prefer a nice, normal looking cat. **(1 point)**

B. Either way is fine with me. (2 points)

C. I want a cat that really stands out. **(3 points)**

· · · · · · · · · · · · · · ·

3 points
A sphynx is not your perfect match.

4–8 points
A sphynx might work. But there might be a better breed for you.

9 points
You and a sphynx would get along well!

athletic (ahth-LEH-tik)—having strong muscles

breed (BREED)—the process by which young animals are produced by their parents; it's also a particular kind of dog, cat, horse, or other animal.

fragile (FRAH-juhl)—easily broken

genetic mutation (juh-NEH-tik mwu-TAY-shun)—a change in a living thing's DNA; DNA is acids in cells that create the traits, qualities, or features of a person, animal, or plant.

infection (in-FEK-shun)—a disease caused by germs that enter the body

oil (OYL)—a greasy liquid substance

unique (yoo-NEEK)—very special or unusual

BOOKS

Felix, Rebecca. *Sphynx.* Cool Cats. Minneapolis: Bellwether Media, 2016.

Furstinger, Nancy, and John Willis. *Sphynx Cats.* All about Cats. New York: AV2 by Weigl, 2018.

Schuh, Mari. *Sphynx Cats.* Favorite Cat Breeds. Mankato, MN: Amicus High Interest, Amicus Ink, 2017.

WEBSITES

All about Sphynx Cats
www.aspcapetinsurance.com/blog/2017/april/17/ sphynx-cat-breed-information/

Breed Profile: The Sphynx
cfa.org/Breeds/BreedsSthruT/Sphynx.aspx

Sphynx
www.animalplanet.com/tv-shows/cats-101/videos/ sphynx

INDEX